THIS BOOK BELONGS TO:

WHO WAS

BORN
TO BE
AWESOME

This book is dedicated to every boy who has ever doubted his courage, his flyness & his strength! Be free!

To my grandad, uncle, brother & cousins & all my loving friends!

Visit us on the Web! rhcbooks.com

Educators and librarians, for a variety of teaching tools, visit us at RHTeachersLibrarians.com

Library of Congress Cataloging-in-Publication Data
Name: Roe, Mechal Renee, author, illustrator.
Title: Cool cuts / written & illustrated by Mechal Renee Roe.
Description: New York : Doubleday Books for Young Readers, [2020] | "Originally self-published in slightly different form in 2016."
Summary: "An illustrated, joyful celebration of African American boys' hairstyles" —Provided by publisher.
Identifiers: LCCN 2018053213 (print) | LCCN 2018057378 (ebook)
ISBN 978-1-9848-9557-8 (hc) | ISBN 978-1-9848-9558-5 (glb) | ISBN 978-1-9848-9559-2 (ebk)
Subjects: | CYAC: Stories in rhyme. | Hair—Fiction. | Hairstyles—Fiction. | African Americans—Fiction. | Self-esteem—Fiction.
Classification: LCC PZ8.3.R6185 (ebook) | LCC PZ8.3.R6185 Coo 2020 (print) | DDC [E]—dc23

MANUFACTURED IN CHINA
10 9 8 7 6 5 4 3

COOL CUTS

Written & illustrated by MECHAL RENEE ROE

Doubleday Books for Young Readers

BORN
AWESOME

WHEN THE STARS SHINE, THE WORLD IS MINE!

i am born to be AWESOME!

I CAN DO ANY TASK— JUST ASK!

i am born to be AWESOME!

MY HAIR IS FREE, JUST LIKE ME!

i am born to be AWESOME!

COOLER THAN MOST!
TRY NOT TO BOAST!

i am born to be AWESOME!

BOOM, BOOM! PLAY MY FAVE TUNES!

i am born to be AWESOME!

BE THE BEST, NO MATTER HOW HARD THE TEST!

i am born to be AWESOME!

TRY, TRY AGAIN!
NEXT TIME, I WIN!

i am born to be AWESOME!

I AM A STAR!
I WORK HARD!

i am born to be AWESOME!

CLEVER & SMART!
I LOVE ART!

i am born to be AWESOME!

A HAPPY BOY, FULL OF JOY!

i am born to be AWESOME!

SO FRESH & SO CLEAN!
READY FOR MY DREAMS!

i am born to be AWESOME!

IF I THINK IT, I CAN ACHIEVE IT!

i am born to be AWESOME!

I AM BORN TO BE AWESOME

HAPPY HAIR®